PRINCESS
Kim
and too much truth

To Kayla—
Warm wishes—
♥ Maryann Cocca-Leffler 2011

By MARYANN COCCA-LEFFLER

Albert Whitman & Company, Chicago, Illinois

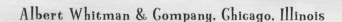

Room
312
JASON
A
helmet
trade
someday
rocket
near
edge
front
above
Kim
helmit X
trade
someday
rocket
near
edge
front
above
B+
Sara
hELMET
TRADE
SomEday
rocket
neer X
edGE
FronT
ABOVE
B+

Today's lesson
HONESTY

At school Mrs. Della talked about telling the truth. "It's important to be honest," she said. "Sometimes telling the truth is hard, but it's the right thing to do."

That night, Kim looked around her room and thought about her name.

Ever since she was born, her family had called her "Princess," but she wasn't a *real* princess. It was time to pack up the pink.

"From now on, no matter what, I'm only going to tell the truth!" Kim announced at breakfast.

"That sounds like a good plan, Princess," said Dad.

"Dad, please don't call me Princess anymore! Truthfully, I'm not!" said Kim.

"Right," said Dad. "Truth only!"
"And by the way—your pancakes
are sort of rubbery," said Kim.
Dad looked surprised. "They are?"

"Have a good day, Kim," said Grandma Betty as she primped in the hall mirror. "Do you like my new necklace? It's handmade."

Kim looked up. She had to tell the truth.

"Ummm . . . it looks just like those slimy rocks from the bottom of my fishtank."

Grandma Betty frowned.
"I think it's pretty."

Grandma Betty handed Kim her princess backpack. "I don't need that. I'm taking everything in this plain brown paper bag. Truthfully, it's much more me," said Kim. "In fact, I'm getting rid of all my princess stuff."

"But you've always been a princess," said Grandma Betty. "Not anymore," said Kim.

Kim got on the school bus. Samantha was draped over the seat in a supermodel pose. "Well? What do you think?"
Kim's eyes widened. "Wow! You have a new hairstyle. It . . ."

Then the truth spilled out.

"It reminds me of Fifi, my Aunt Mary's poodle!"

Samantha sat up.
"Well, everyone else likes it!"

Nice
boots

Very
stylish

Awesome

Wow!

When Kim got to the schoolyard, everyone was admiring Violet's new boots. They were covered with orange and green frogs.

"Aren't these the coolest boots you've ever seen?" asked Violet.

Kim looked closer.

"I hate frogs," Kim said.

Cool

Violet looked shocked. "How can anyone hate frogs?"
"It's the truth," said Kim.

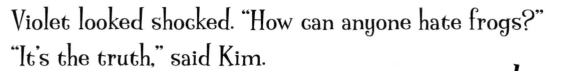

"But I think frogs are great! They can
jump in puddles—just like this!" said Violet.

As they walked into the classroom, Mrs. Della followed with a mop. "Who's tracking mud on the floor?"

Out of Kim's mouth came more truth.

"It's Violet and her frog boots."

Everyone stared at Kim.
"Tattletale!" said Abby.
"Well, I can't lie," said Kim.

"From now on I'm only telling the truth."

And Kim told the truth all morning.

In music class, when the teacher introduced them to classical music, Kim said,

"It's so boring I'm falling asleep."

In art class, when Sara showed Kim her wire sculpture, Kim said,

"It looks like moldy spaghetti."

"Oh," said Sara sadly.

Then the class shared their
poetry paintings. Everyone
tacked a painting on the board.
Kevin went first and read:
"Blast off high
    to touch the sky.
Fly so far—
    touch a star."

The kids all clapped. "Great job," said Mrs. Della.
She turned to the class. "Any comments?"

"I like your costume,"
said Justin.

"I love the purple sky,"
commented Violet.

Kim took a long look at the painting. She had to tell the truth.

"No one can touch a star, and you're NOT really an astronaut!"

Mrs. Della gave Kim a stern look. She made a "zip your mouth" motion.

Kim zipped her mouth. She looked at Kevin. He had his head down.

Kim thought hard. She didn't get it. She'd told the truth, hadn't she?

"I was *pretending* to be an astronaut . . . like you pretend to be a princess," said Kevin. "It's just for fun."

Just then there was a commotion in the back of the classroom. Everyone was "oohing" and "aahing."

"Kim! Come see! Mrs. Bell is visiting with her brand-new baby!" called Riley.

Kim followed.

"She is sooo cute!" cooed Jason.

"Look at those tiny fingers," said Samantha.

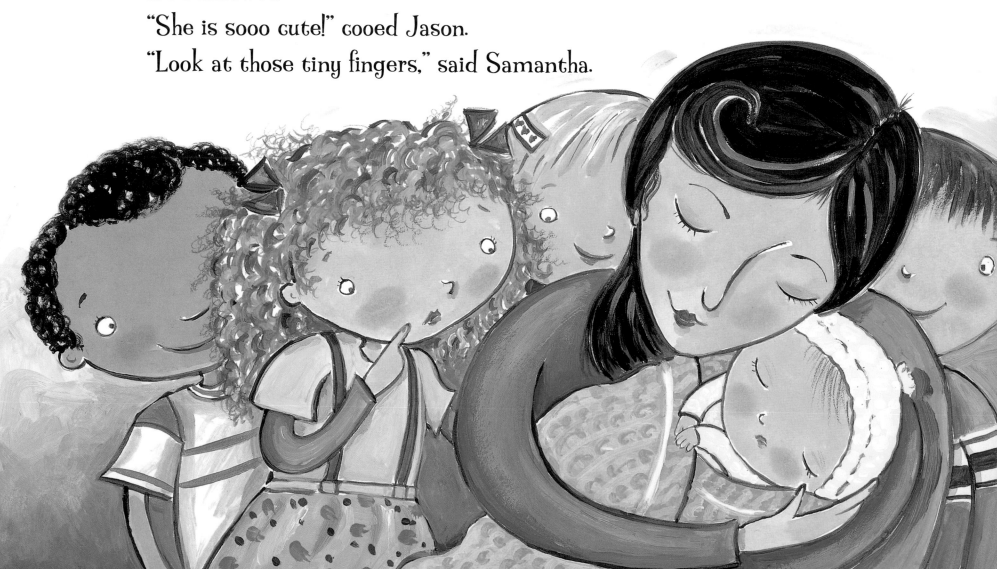

Kim just stood there, staring.

The baby was squishy, and drooling, and making funny faces.

"What do you think, Kim? Isn't she adorable?" asked Mrs. Bell.

Kim closed her eyes. She tried to keep her mouth zipped. But out came the truth . . .

"That is the ugliest baby I

Did she just say that?

Oh, my!

Mrs. Della came running over.
"Who started this ruckus?" she asked.
No one said a word.
Kim knew that she had to tell the truth.
Softly she said,

"I did."

Mrs. Della took Kim aside. "What's going on with you today?"

Kim looked up. "Yesterday you told us how important it is to be honest—to tell the truth."

"Yes, I did. Telling the truth is very important—"

"But telling the truth is what caused the ruckus!" interrupted Kim. "I told the truth. I told Mrs. Bell that her baby was kind of . . . ummm . . . ugly."

"Oh, Kim," Mrs. Della said. "Telling the truth doesn't mean you say everything you're thinking. You might hurt people's feelings."

The class settled down for snacks. Kim sat next to Violet.

"Telling the truth is just not working out," said Kim. "All the kids hate me."

"To tell the truth—I don't like Kevin's painting, either," whispered Violet.

"You said you did," said Kim. "You lied!"

"I didn't lie," explained Violet. "I said, 'I love the purple sky,' and I do. Purple is my favorite color. After all, my name *is* Violet. I didn't want to hurt Kevin's feelings, so I told him 'one single thing' I liked about his painting."

"*One Single Thing*. That's a good idea," said Kim. "It's not lying at all, and it doesn't hurt anyone's feelings."

Kim looked at Violet's boots.
"Well, I don't like the frogs on
your boots, but I do like the way
you can jump in puddles. And
that's the truth."
Violet smiled.

Kim turned to Kevin.
"Kevin—I like the spaceship
in your painting. It makes me
want to fly to the moon."
"Thanks," said Kevin.

Then Kim walked over to the baby.

"I'm sorry, Mrs. Bell." Kim got closer. "I think your baby smells nice, like flowers."

"That's kind of you," said Mrs. Bell. "The truth is, she doesn't always smell nice! But we focus on the good things. Would you like to hold her?"

"Sure," said Kim.

That night Kim told Grandma Betty about her day.
"You know, Grandma," Kim said, "I really like
the colors in your fishtank-rock necklace."
"Thank you," said Grandma Betty.
Kim looked at the box of princess stuff.
"And Grandma, can I still pretend
to be a princess sometimes?
It's not lying."

"You sure can,"
said Grandma Betty.
"Princess Kim, let's
unpack the pink!"

YIPPEE!

To Mom and Dad,
who have always shown kindness and love.
With love,
Maryann

Library of Congress Cataloging-in-Publication Data

Cocca-Leffler, Maryann, 1958-
Princess Kim and too much truth / by Maryann Cocca-Leffler.
p. cm.
Summary: Young Kim discovers that there is a difference between being honest
and always speaking the truth.
ISBN 978-0-8075-6618-3
[1. Honesty–Fiction. 2. Behavior–Fiction. 3. Schools–Fiction.] I. Title.
PZ7.C638Psk 2011 [E]–dc22 2010024275

The design is by Maryann Cocca-Leffler and Carol Gildar.

For more information about Albert Whitman & Company, please visit our web site at www.albertwhitman.com.

Please visit Maryann at her web site: www.maryanncoccaleffler.com.